SALLY RIDE AND THE NEW ASTRONAUTS

SALLY RIDE

AND

THE NEW

ASTRONAUTS

SCIENTISTS IN SPACE

BY
KAREN O'CONNOR

A GROLIER COMPANY

FRANKLIN WATTS 1983
New York | London | Toronto | Sydney

To Clarissa,
with affection

The author wishes to thank
the National Aeronautics and Space Administration
for photographs and assistance in preparing this book.

Photographs courtesy of NASA

Library of Congress Cataloging in Publication Data

O'Connor, Karen.
Sally Ride and the new astronauts.

Includes index.
Summary: Describes the experiences of the first
American woman astronaut, scheduled to travel in space
in 1983, and explains how astronauts are selected
and trained and how it feels to fly in space.
1. Astronautics—United States—Juvenile literature.
2. Ride, Sally—Juvenile literature. 3. Astronauts—
United States—Biography—Juvenile literature.
(1. Astronauts. 2. Ride, Sally. 3. Astronautics.
4. Space flight. 5. Space flight training) I. Title.
TL793.028 1983   629.45′07   82-21844
ISBN 0-531-04602-8

CONTENTS

SALLY RIDE AND
THE NEW ASTRONAUTS

Sally Ride and Rhea Seddon (blonde hair), another astronaut in training, practice ocean-survival exercises at Homestead Air Force Base in Florida. The course is designed to teach trainees what to do in the event of an emergency ejection from the shuttle over water.

CLOSE ENCOUNTER
WITH SALLY RIDE

"What am I doing here?" Sally Ride asked herself, bobbing around on a tiny raft in the choppy waters off south Florida. " I'm supposed to be a smart person."

It was August 1978, and the young astronaut-in-training was beginning to find out what her new career was all about. She and her classmates, all members of the National Aeronautics and Space Administration's (NASA's) eighth astronaut-training class, had begun the physical part of their program. For three days the group would practice special ocean-survival exercises. Before the session was over, trainers would hook the pretty, dark-haired astronaut by rope to a motorboat, then drag her backward through Biscayne Bay and drop her 400 feet (120 m) into the salty ocean. They would then send her down a 45-foot (13.5-m) tower into water infested with mosquitoes.

This was a new form of activity for athletic Sally Ride, quite different from jogging, volleyball, or rugby. And it was nothing at all like tennis, at one time her favorite sport.

ADVENTURE OF A LIFETIME None of this stopped Sally from going ahead with her plans to become an astronaut, though. Like most people in the program, she has a natural love of adventure.

"Thirty years from now," she said, "when they're selling round-trip tickets to Mars, this (being an astronaut)

[1

might not be glamorous, but right now it's a once-in-a-lifetime opportunity."

FIRST AMERICAN WOMAN IN SPACE Four years later, NASA would give Sally a second once-in-a-lifetime opportunity. In April 1982, she would be selected to be the first American woman in space. Her mission would take place in April 1983. She and three other astronauts would be on a six-day mission aboard the space shuttle *Challenger*. At age thirty-one, Sally would be the youngest American astronaut ever to go into orbit, in addition to being the first woman. Her training off the Florida coast had been designed to teach her how to handle herself in an emergency situation should she encounter one during her flight.

Today, Sally is a celebrity. But she has remained a very private person. She doesn't like interviews and prefers to keep the details of her personal life out of the news and separate from her work.

At the same time, she is known for her lively sense of humor and cool manner. "I'm very honored NASA chose me to be the first woman," Sally told a group of reporters after the announcement came. Then she quickly added that she was more excited to have the chance to go into space than to be the first woman to do so.

More than 8,000 people, including 1,544 women, applied to become astronauts the same time Sally Ride did. NASA accepted only 35 candidates altogether. Six were women—Sally Ride, Rhea Seddon, Anna Fisher, Shannon Lucid, Judith Resnik, and Kathryn Sullivan. In 1980, two more women, Mary Cleave and Bonnie Dunbar, were accepted.

"At first," said Sally, "I was worried that NASA might be setting out to choose a token woman. But out of the thirty-five chosen, six were women. That's not tokenism. I believe that one-third of the scientists at NASA are women."

Sally has progressed quickly in her astronaut training since she was accepted into the program in 1978. Captain Robert L. Crippen, commander of the mission she will go on, said she had become a fine engineer.

This "Women in Space" NASA poster features the eight
women who are now part of NASA's astronaut corps.
Clockwise, from upper left, are Mary Cleave, Bonnie
Dunbar, Judith Resnik, Anna Fisher, Kathyrn Sullivan,
Rhea Seddon, Sally Ride, and Shannon Lucid.

FROM TENNIS NUT TO ASTRONAUT

Sally's parents, Dale and Joyce Ride, don't claim to know exactly how or why Sally made the shuttle team. But they do admit that their daughter has always been athletic and competitive.

Sports were an important part of Sally's childhood. While growing up in Encino, California, the freckle-faced little girl never backed away from a good game of football or baseball. And much of the time this meant playing with boys only.

Mr. Ride recalled that as young as age five, his daughter raced him for the daily sports page. "She knows what she can do, and she likes to win," he told a reporter for the *Los Angeles Times*.

Winning in competition is not new to Sally. In 1969, while attending Swarthmore College, she won a national tennis tournament for college students. Later, as a student at Stanford University, she played on the women's rugby team.

Sally Ride was an outstanding student and always received excellent grades. But she was a normal kid at the same time. If she was bored in the classroom or didn't like what was being taught, she'd stop paying attention. "It irritated some teachers," Sally's mother said. "One saw her as a clock-watcher. That was the one exception. She was dull, and Sally was bored."

FROM WORLD TRAVELER TO SPACE TRAVELER

Sally has learned a lot from her parents, too. Both are active in their community and church. Mr. Ride works as the assistant to the superintendent of Santa Monica College. Mrs. Ride does volunteer work in a women's prison. In the past, she has taught English to foreign-speaking students. The Rides are also elders in the Encino Presbyterian Church.

In 1960, young Sally and her sister Karen, now a minister, spent a year traveling through Europe with their parents. Dale Ride took a sabbatical from his work at the college. The family used his time off to tour several countries. They studied various governments and educational systems and enjoyed the sights.

For Sally and Karen Ride, aged nine and seven, a whole new world opened up that year. Subways, hotel rooms, and unusual foods fascinated the two girls.

Back in the United States, the sisters continued to meet people from all over the world. Their parents belonged to the World Affairs Council's visitors program. They often invited official foreign visitors to stay in their home.

HEAD START IN PHYSICS In 1968, Sally graduated from the Westlake School for Girls in Los Angeles. She remembers her physics teacher, Elizabeth Mommaerts, as one of the most important influences on her life. According to the school's headmaster, Nathan Reynolds, the woman was "an extraordinary teacher" and a very special human being.

"I wanted to be an astronaut as a child," Sally told a reporter for the *Saturday Evening Post,* "but I never thought it was possible." Yet the little girl did not let go of her dream in the years following. Perhaps her teacher, Ms. Mommaerts, somehow inspired Sally to keep after it.

If becoming an astronaut turned out to be impossible, Sally decided, at least she would work in some area of the space program. Thus, in college, she continued her studies in physics and astrophysics (a branch of astronomy concerned with the composition of celestial objects). And while dreaming of becoming one of the first women to travel in space, she became a top-ranking college tennis player.

In 1969, a reporter for the *Delaware County Daily Times* in Pennsylvania called Sally the number one female college tennis player in the East. Later in the article, the reporter mentioned that Sally said she would one day like to work for NASA, and she "hopes she has what it takes to make a space team."

MAKING THE TEAM Nine years later, while studying for her doctorate degree in astrophysics at Stanford University, Sally found out that she indeed had what it took. A telephone call from the Johnson Space Center in Houston, Texas, woke her from a sound sleep. "I wasn't sure it was really Houston," Sally later told a reporter. "Now I'm so excited, I'd like to go up (into space) tomorrow."

Before taking off for the heavens, however, the young astrophysicist had some business to take care of. She had to pack up her belongings and clear out of her apartment. She also had to clean out her campus office in the Physics Department at Stanford, where she had been a research assistant.

READY TO FLY Since 1978, Sally has completed her basic astronaut training and has also served as capsule communicator for the second and third flights of the space shuttle *Columbia.* As the "capcom," Sally was the only person at the Mission Operations Control Center in Houston to talk to the astronauts while they were in flight.

During the second flight, which took place in November 1981, one of the astronauts described how the earth looked to him from the towering point of 150 miles (240 km) up. Sally radioed her reply to crewmen Joe Engle and Richard Truly. "Sounds good," she said. "When do I get my chance?" April 1983 would have been the correct answer, but few people, including Sally, knew it then.

Sally is now ready for that flight, her first in space. Long hours of training and classroom work were needed for her to learn her particular duties for the six-day mission.

As the *Challenger* rises into orbit, then later reenters the earth's atmosphere and lands, Sally will act as flight engineer. During these times, she will assist spacecraft commander Robert Crippen and pilot Frederick Hauck. For example, she will help monitor the glowing cockpit lights and gauges that tell the pilots how the flight is going.

For the rest of the six-day mission, Sally Ride and Air Force Lieutenant Colonel John Fabian will work together as mission specialists. Their job will consist mainly of working with three satellites that will be placed into orbit. They will also be responsible for carrying out the scientific experiments scheduled for that flight.

ROLE MODEL For Sally, there is no doubt that the women's movement has cleared the way for her career in space. She was able to move from university life into the space program without losing a step. The women's movement had advanced just ahead of her. By the time Sally decided

Astronauts Joe Engle (left) and Richard Truly, the crew of the
second flight of the *Columbia*, are shown here training in
the shuttle mission simulator at the Johnson Space Center.

The crew for the seventh mission of the space shuttle program and the second flight of the *Challenger* are shown here following a news conference. From left to right: Frederick Hauck, Robert Crippen, Sally Ride, and John Fabian.

to apply for a job as an astronaut, the space agency had already announced that women would be admitted into the program.

Sally and the other women in the astronaut corps now speak at high schools and colleges about once a month. Students crowd around Sally after she talks. "When I go out and give talks at schools, and an eight-year-old girl in the audience raises her hand to ask me what she needs to do to become an astronaut, I like that," said Sally. "It's neat! Because now there really is a way. Now it's possible!"

Their talks with students have made all of the female astronauts aware that they are truly role models for young women all over the country. Perhaps even more important than their actual work in space, they are showing today's young people how they, too, can live their dream.

2

A NEW KIND OF ASTRONAUT

"We have selected an outstanding group of women and men, who represent the most competent, talented, and experienced people available to us today," said NASA administrator Dr. Robert A. Froesch. He was referring to NASA's eighth class of astronauts, selected in 1978.

The class of thirty-five included two Europeans, three blacks, one Hispanic, and six women. This was a real change from former classes, where only military-trained test pilots were considered. Astronauts of the future will also include middle-aged as well as young people, pilots and nonpilots, and scientists and technicians.

SPECIALISTS —DOING THEIR OWN THING
As many as five mission specialists can go along on a space shuttle flight. They will have little to do with the flying. Trained pilots will fly the craft into orbit and back to earth. Meanwhile, the mission specialists will operate experimental equipment, study the planets, sun, or other stars, or keep watch on the health of the crew.

The eight women currently trained as astronauts will all be mission specialists. Part of their responsibilities will be to check out satellites and deploy them. These satellites help us to learn more about the weather, landmasses, water resources, pollution, and also aid in defense and communications.

Foreign governments, private businesses, private organizations, and even private citizens can, for a fee,

Part of the astronaut class of '78. Third row back, on the far right, is Steven Hawley, later to become the husband of Sally Ride.

have their experiments conducted by an astronaut while in orbit. Many have already done so.

According to one magazine report, Stephen Spielberg, who directed *E.T. The Extra-Terrestrial* and *Close Encounters of the Third Kind,* is considering becoming one of the shuttle program's customers. Could he be gathering some new ideas for his next film?

Young people can also send experiments on a mission as part of the Student Involvement Project. The experiment must be safe, travel in a container, and not take up too much of the astronaut's time.

TRAINING AND LEARNING Training chief James Bilodeau says the new breed of astronauts are being trained for two kinds of flights. One is the kind in which astronauts deploy (leave) a payload (cargo) in orbit. The other involves monitoring equipment sent up with the shuttle. Most of the missions will be "deploys" he says. For example, on Sally Ride's mission, she and John Fabian will be carrying out a scientific experiment belonging to West Germany and deploying communications satellites for Canada and Indonesia.

On long missions, mission specialists may also work with special instruments and cameras that will remain permanently attached to the shuttle. They will be in charge of aiming that equipment toward the earth or outer space for various experiments.

Right now, only a few astronauts are doing specialized work. Most are capable of doing many different jobs. They work as engineers, scientists, and researchers. They also learn how to fly and operate the shuttle. Their training and testing program is very exciting. But it involves a lot of plain hard work, too.

The astronauts of the eighties are doing many more things than the astronauts of the past. Some people think they sit in classrooms all day or train only in fancy simulators. "But we do almost none of that," said Mission Specialist Tony England. In fact, there is only one shuttle mission simulator located in Houston, and it is used almost exclusively to train astronauts for the next scheduled mission. The rest of the astronauts learn in other ways.

In 1980, for example, Tony England worked with a team of astronauts whose job it was to help test the shuttle orbiter's instruments and controls. Sometimes testing continued twenty-four hours a day seven days a week. Tony often sat in the cockpit for twelve hours at a time.

These long hours of testing gave him more flying experience than any other astronaut, even those assigned to missions. By the time Tony begins orbital flights, he'll be ready to take emergency control of the orbiter if necessary.

WOMEN IN SPACE A big change in the astronaut program came in 1978, when the first women were admitted. "Everybody wondered what changes it would make and whether or not the women could cut it," said one official. The wondering didn't last very long. It soon became clear that the women chosen knew as much as or more than the men.

"We've got women here who are better engineers than some of the men," said Alan Bean, former head of the astronaut office. And they have shown that they can keep physically fit, too.

The officials at NASA were not the only ones who were delighted at how well the women did. The women themselves were. "When I came here," said Sally Ride, "I had no idea what this life would be like.

"I'm an astrophysicist," said Sally, talking about her reasons for becoming an astronaut. "There are direct and obvious experiments in my field, such as X-ray and infrared astronomy, that can't be done in an earth-bound observatory."

Since 1978, Sally has learned quickly. Before being assigned as a mission specialist on the *Challenger,* she worked at many jobs in the space program. She and two electrical engineers, astronauts Judy Resnik and William Lenoir, helped to test the shuttle's Remote Manipulator System. The manipulator is the huge robotic arm that can lift satellites out of the orbiter and bring them back again. It was designed and built in Canada. When the manipulator was first tested in space in November 1981, Sally assisted from Mission Control.

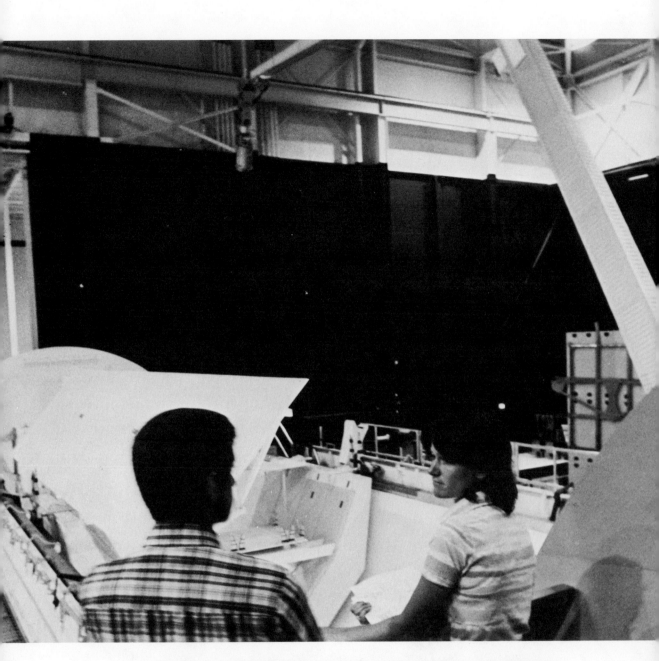

Mission specialists Terry Bart and Sally Ride participate
in a simulation session with a model of the shuttle's
remote manipulator arm. Note the arm in the top portion
of the picture. Below it is a model of the shuttle's huge
cargo bay area, shown with its "clamshell" doors open.

Two astronauts run through a training session in the shuttle's mission simulator at the Mission Simulation and Training Facility at the Johnson Space Center.

In April 1982 she acted as capsule communicator for the shuttle *Columbia.* She was the first woman to do so.

Before a mission, Sally and the other astronauts on the team learn all about the shuttle by training in a simulator, or model, many hours a week. "It's another way to learn about the orbiter systems," Sally told a reporter. By using the simulator they also learn how to identify and solve problems and how to keep things running smoothly during a normal flight. "We have one full-scale simulation every week lasting eight to ten hours," said Sally.

Shannon Lucid, one of the other female astronauts named in 1978, was part of the team Tony England headed. She is not a rated jet pilot. But like Tony, she, too, has had enough practice in the simulator so that she could bring the orbiter back to earth if she had to.

Commenting on the shuttle, electrical engineer Judith Resnik said, "Progress in science is as exciting to me as sitting in a rocket is to some people. I feel less like Columbus and more like Galileo."

Anna Fisher and her astronaut-husband, William Fisher, are medical doctors. They specialize in emergency care. Joining the space program is something Anna has always wanted to do. "As a species we need to go one step beyond where we are," she said in an interview. "We need a frontier. Without it, I think life would be very confining."

Today, Anna and Bill Fisher's lives are anything but confining. As physicians, they are expected to keep up with their medical practice in addition to their astronaut training. The husband-wife team spend at least one weekend day each month in a hospital emergency room. They also take turns as recovery-room doctors at Edwards Air Force Base or at the landing strip in New Mexico during shuttle missions.

During the last two years, Anna has also helped perfect the highly mobile shuttle space suit and the unique shuttle "rescue ball." An astronaut from a disabled orbiter could hang onto the rescue ball while another astronaut carried it to a second shuttle waiting nearby.

Above: Anna Fisher, seen here wearing the shuttle
space suit during training at the Johnson Space
Center. *Opposite:* Robert Williams, of Johnson's
Crew Systems Division, is shown here suited up and
standing beside the proposed shuttle "rescue ball."

NASA assigned Anna's husband, Bill, to ride in the back seat of a B-57 aircraft conducting high-altitude research. Bill said that he and his wife were beginning to feel a little like traveling salespeople. "One week I'm on the road, and the next week Anna's gone," he said.

Rhea Seddon is also a physician. She is a surgeon with a special interest in surgical nutrition—feeding people by injecting liquids directly into the bloodstream. "This is a brand-new field of medicine," said Rhea, "and I think this specialization made me interesting to the space program. Also, anyone who has an M.D. has a wide scientific background."

The youngest female astronaut is Kathryn Sullivan. She was twenty-six when NASA chose her for the program. "My field is marine geophysics," said Kathryn. "The part I am really looking forward to is walking in space." Since she is an earth scientist, the idea of being able to look back at the earth from orbit is very exciting. "I'd also love to do more space exploration," she added.

EQUAL OPPORTUNITY Like Sally Ride, Shannon Lucid believes that the opportunity for women in space came from the women's movement. With the push for equal opportunity in all kinds of jobs, more and more organizations began to hire women.

During the 1970s, several female scientists started planning for the time when women would be accepted into the space program. They began developing specialties that could be used by NASA. Dr. Mary Helen Johnston, a metallurgical engineer, Ann Whitaker, a specialist in surface physics, and Carolyn Griner, an astronautical engineer, taught themselves many things. For example, they flew low-gravity arcs in aircraft and learned what they could and could not do in a nearly weightless environment.

Dr. Johnston told a writer for the magazine *Space World,* "I am convinced that a woman could do any job a man could do on a space flight, if we are allowed to go." Early in 1978, NASA chose the first group of female astronauts.

As more women go into work that was at one time "for men only," society will gradually accept the change. But in the meantime, women themselves must take the initiative and work for change.

"They must prepare themselves, professionally, for the coming opportunities in space exploration," said Charles Boyle in an article for *Space World* in 1978.

Shannon Lucid, astronaut as well as mother of three children, did just that. "I was about a fifth- or sixth-grader when I decided I wanted to be an astronaut," she said. "A long time before America even had a manned space program, I was very interested in space flight. I was just hoping the government would get interested."

Shannon planned her education carefully. She earned degrees in chemistry and biochemistry and then got a job at the Oklahoma Medical Research Foundation.

"I've always been interested in space," said Shannon, who is a perfect example of a person who knew what she wanted to do, prepared herself to do it, and was ready to step in when the opportunity came along.

The smallest of the female astronauts, 5-feet 2-inch (2-m) Mary Cleave, tried to get into aviation as a first step toward her career in space. But things just didn't go as planned. "They said I couldn't be a stewardess and that actually I was too short to even sell tickets," Mary recalled.

At that point she grew discouraged but decided to keep trying to fulfill her dream of joining the space program. Her next step was to take flying lessons. She also earned two doctoral degrees in engineering. NASA chose her for the program in the summer of 1980.

"They picked me in case they ever had a job for a midget," Mary joked. In a more serious moment, she added, "The early astronauts were the explorers. We are the homesteaders."

The Soviet Union has also given their women opportunities in the space program. In 1963 Valentina Tereshkova beame the first female to join the Russian space team. She flew a 48-orbit mission aboard *Vostok-6*.

More recently, in August 1982, just eight months before Sally Ride's flight, Moscow's thirty-four-year-old Svetlana Savitskaya ("Sveta") became the second

Soviet woman to go into orbit and return safely. Sveta, who was an award-winning parachutist and pilot as a teenager, flew aboard the space vehicle *Soyuz T-7*. While in orbit, she carried out a busy schedule of experiments in astrophysics, space metallurgy, and more. According to reports, however, the Soviet Union was primarily interested in seeing how well Savitskaya could adapt to weightlessness.

WORKING TOGETHER Teamwork is an important part of the "new" astronaut program. The shuttle will be carrying crews of up to seven men and women. A successful mission depends on complete cooperation during the long hours before the launch and during the flight itself. As Rhea Seddon put it, "On the shuttle we are and we have to be more team players."

Bonnie Dunbar, one of the more recently chosen women, thinks that having to work so intently with the other astronauts is part of the fun. "We really have to like each other a lot to work closely in space and to be up there together so much," she said.

The new astronauts often spend time together when they're not at work. Many are close friends. Sally Ride's parents, who have met most of the astronauts, described them to a reporter for the *Los Angeles Times* as "a fascinating group of young people, well-qualified, all dedicated, and a lot of fun. They play a lot."

GETTING AN ASSIGNMENT One of the most exciting moments in an astronaut's life is being assigned to his or her first spaceflight. Exactly how the crew members for each mission are chosen is not known.

NASA's training program is unique. It is not at all like college, or military training. An astronaut no longer has to be a test pilot. And being a brilliant student in the classroom is not the only thing that counts.

"Successful astronauts know how to win out," says Alan Bean, who has worked with many groups of astronauts. They don't need to be excessively competitive. They notice what others do and imitate those at the top.

Competition might have been more keen in the early days of space travel, when only one or two astronauts were needed for each flight. Today, good teamwork is more important.

Robert Crippen has been an astronaut since 1969. He did not go into space until chosen as copilot for the April 1982 flight of the *Columbia.* Soon, however, he'll make his second trip into space. This time he will be commander of the *Challenger,* on the same mission that will carry Sally Ride into space.

The new astronauts will not have to wait that long for their turn. As the shuttle era of space travel intensifies, larger crews will be needed. Thirty-one shuttle flights are planned between September 1982 and August 1985. Many people will go into space with them. Some astronauts will have the chance to fly on more than one mission during that time.

A STAR AMONG THE STARS One big difference between the old and new astronauts is public attention. Astronauts of the 1980s will probably not be as famous as the men of the Gemini and Apollo programs. In the early days of space travel, astronauts such as John Glenn and Neil Armstrong became national heroes.

The astronauts of the shuttle era, however, don't expect to be in hometown parades or on the front page of national newspapers. Many of them will go into space over the next several years. And within twenty years, spaceflights may become quite common. As they become more routine, public attention will probably settle down. The first American woman in space, Sally Ride, and the first black, Guion Bluford, Jr., may be the last astronauts to be treated as "stars."

Most of the astronauts are happy they will not receive a lot of publicity. Kathryn Sullivan, a member of the same class as Sally Ride, is one example. In 1981, a few months before Sally was selected, Kathryn told a reporter, "I wouldn't mind being the first woman in space, but I think it might even be better to be the second one. Then I would be less famous and could return to the scientific work more quickly."

Sally Ride stands beside Guion Bluford, Jr.,
following a press conference announcing their
missions. Bluford, a lieutenant colonel in the
Air Force, will be the first black person in space.
His flight will directly follow Sally Ride's.

THE PUBLIC'S RIGHT TO KNOW

In the past, public attention has sometimes interfered with an astronaut's personal life. But the new astronauts are less likely to have that problem. Most of their training takes place in Houston, Texas. During this time, the astronauts are pretty much off-limits to television and news reporters. And because there are more of them now, interest in their personal lives has dwindled.

Sally Ride has been the exception. As the first American woman in space, everyone wants to talk to her, ask her questions, and find out what she's like. Even her parents have been called by hundreds of people. But Sally continues to be a private person.

Some reporters called her cold and difficult. They feel she will hurt the space program if she doesn't soften her attitude.

John Lawrence of NASA's public affairs office told one reporter that the astronauts do not have to do anything they don't want to. NASA doesn't dictate to them. "Some of them guard their private lives," he said. Sally Ride is one who does.

This can cause problems, though. Astronauts do have a right to their personal lives. On the other hand, citizens have a right to know something about these pioneers in space and anyone else whose work they support with their tax dollars.

If they had their way, the eight female astronauts would be treated just like the men in the program. They think of themselves as ordinary people who just happen to have very interesting jobs. "We do the same work as the men," said Shannon Lucid, "yet nobody asks them about how their kids feel about their work."

Rhea Seddon, who married astronaut Robert Gibson in 1981, had her first baby recently. She is the first female astronaut to give birth while still active in the space program. But Rhea refuses to be considered special. Speaking for Shannon and herself she said, "We have the same problems as any working mother."

Anna and Bill Fisher would like to have a family someday, but for now they are totally committed to their work as astronauts. As for Sally Ride, she sees no problem in this area for herself. "The space program is going to have absolutely no effect on my plans for marriage or

Sally Ride is seen here going over some post-flight data from a debriefing session given by the astronauts from the third shuttle mission.

anything else," she said. And apparently it hasn't. On July 24, 1982, Sally married thirty-year-old fellow astronaut Steven Hawley in a quiet service at Steven's father's home in Kansas.

The two met in 1978, while they were both in training for the space program. Steven is a graduate of the University of California, where he earned a PhD in astronomy and astrophysics.

A JOB LIKE ANY OTHER In the early days of the space program, most of the astronauts dropped out when their chances of flying became slim. They went on to other careers, including politics and business. The new astronauts, however, can look forward to a long career in space, if they choose it. As more and more flights are scheduled, and space travel becomes truly routine, there will be plenty of work for anyone who wants to make a career of it.

At the same time, an astronaut's life is not an easy one. In fact, it is more challenging than ever. Dozens of shuttle missions over the next several years will require extensive planning and training. All of this takes commitment and many hours of work and study.

Those who are dedicated to the space program know what is expected of them. And they're willing to give everything they've got. In fact, more than most, they know what is possible through space technology. Most of them want the program to grow. In the near future, they'd like to see the United States build small space stations and platforms and set up laboratories in earth orbit where experiments and research can be conducted.

These new-age astronauts seem to be more interested in the job than in the glory. Many, in fact, back away from a celebrity role. "The whole point of the shuttle is to make flying into and out of space routine," said one. "There's not much glamour in that."

Maybe not for those who actually do the job. But there are a lot of earthbound folks who still think it's very glamorous to travel in space—even if it is a lot of plain hard work. "There's still an aura about it," says Anna Fisher. "People don't realize it's a job like any other. But once you're involved in the kinds of things we're doing, it has a certain routine."

3

TO THE HEAVENS AND BACK

On July 4, 1982, astronaut Ken Mattingly piloted the space shuttle *Columbia* to a safe and picture-perfect landing in the California desert. It was more than an occasion. It was a celebration. The *Columbia* had successfully completed its fourth and last test flight.

NASA could announce with pride that its newest flying machine was at last ready to go to work full time. The *Columbia* and its sister ships would begin to carry cargo and passengers into space on a regular basis.

NEXT IN LINE As the cheers for the *Columbia* died down, the shuttle *Challenger* stood next in line. Sitting atop a specially designed Boeing 747 airplane, it was all set for a piggyback ride to its new home at Kennedy Space Center in Cape Canaveral, Florida.

Columbia is the first in a parade of shuttles, known collectively as the Space Transportation System (STS). These high-powered space vehicles combine the technology of a rocket and an airplane. The shuttle is the first reusable spacecraft. The *Columbia* is designed to fly one hundred missions or more. This means space travel should eventually cost much less than it does now.

GETTING THE JOB DONE During a magazine interview, astronauts John Young and Robert Crippen, commander and copilot for *Columbia's* maiden voyage, talked about the shuttle and

On July 4, 1982, the *Challenger* was flown
to Florida via Houston to prepare for its
maiden voyage early in 1983.

its amazing abilities. "We'll be able to do in five or ten years what it would take us twenty to thirty years to do otherwise," said Young. "It will absolutely revolutionize the way we do business here on earth."

"There's lots of commercial use being made of space today," said Crippen, "and there's going to be even more in the near future."

Many companies are already signed up to get their satellites on board the space shuttle. "We're filled up now for more years than we can predict what we'll be able to carry," he said. At this time, communications and weather satellites are the most popular payload, or cargo.

Already planned for launching in 1985 is the powerful Space Telescope that will orbit the earth far above the interference of clouds and smog. At a height of 310 miles (496 km), it will give a view of the stars fifty times sharper than anything used on earth.

SPACE FACTORIES The shuttle will also be able to carry into space the materials necessary to build all kinds of structures that people could live and work in. As one astronaut put it, "We could move a fifth of our factories out of earth's environment and into limitless space."

These factories may be able to produce certain chemicals, metals, or other products impossible to make on earth. The first "space factories" could appear within the next few years. They will not be true factories, but they will be a first step toward the real thing. These early space factories will be used for making latex spheres (hard plastic or rubberlike balls) and for manufacturing certain medicines and drugs. At least thirty missions through 1987 will carry gear for processing materials.

Some people still refer to experiments in space as zero-gravity research. But that thinking is beginning to change. The truth is, there is no such thing as zero-gravity. The earth's pull simply gets weaker at greater distances. Scientists call this low gravity (low-g) or microgravity. However, even though there is still some gravity hundreds of miles above the surface of the earth, that gravity is so low that many of the effects that would interfere with experiments or certain processes on the ground disappear.

Many experts believe that by using the shuttle we will be able to improve communications. In fact, Clark Covington, a planner for NASA, says that the shuttle may be able to solve many communications problems.

For example, as it stands now, positions for communications satellites in orbit over the earth are in great demand. Messages via satellite are "switched" on the ground. In other words, transmittal stations on the ground beam signals to the satellite by means of special antennas. The satellites then send the signals back to the earth. Receiving stations in various parts of the world pick up these signals from the transmittal station. This method has created very crowded conditions.

Using the shuttle could change all that. The switching stations could be put in orbit. This would cut down on the number of switching stations needed. And it would offer satellite communications to more customers.

Because the shuttle returns to earth intact, damaged communications satellites could be brought back to earth for repairs, if necessary. This alone could save millions of dollars.

Some scientists say that telephone communications could be beamed directly to the customer. Before long, people may be able to carry wireless telephones with them wherever they go. This may lead to pocket, purse, or even wrist telephones.

The shuttle will also improve television communications. TV signals could be sent to the viewer from space. This would make it possible for TV sets anywhere in the United States to receive dozens of new channels.

Scientists list health care as another major area where the shuttle could make a significant contribution. One of the early experiments will involve the testing of a new treatment for heart disease.

The shuttle may help us to solve other problems, too. It might be used to dispose of nuclear waste in space. Or shuttle crews might build a satellite for capturing energy from the sun and converting it into electricity. And in the near future, it may be possible for meteorologists to predict the weather more accurately than they do now.

"DUMBO, THE SPACE TRUCK" On the launch pad, the shuttle looks like a huge silo with two pointed candles attached to it. The orbiter itself clings to one side.

Actually, the "silo" is a huge tank loaded with 1.6 million gallons (6 million l) of liquid fuel. And the "candles" are powerful solid-fuel rocket engines. Along with the main engines, they thrust the large spacecraft into earth orbit.

To some people, the orbiter itself looks a bit gawky. It seems to lack the sleek design of a modern airship. As a result, it has earned the playful nickname, "Dumbo, the space truck."

Up to seven astronauts can ride in the shuttle. They live and work in a double-deck cabin. The rest of the craft is a 60-foot-long (18-m) cargo bay that can hold as much as 65,000 pounds (29,250 kg). The shuttle is launched by rocket engines but returns to land on a runway, like an airplane.

The space shuttle's orbiter is the most advanced spacecraft in the world. Its three main engines are far more complex than the engines that sent the *Apollos* to the moon.

Building the world's most sophisticated rocket was no small job. It was a long process involving the latest technology. The space shuttle's main engines were put together in Canoga Park, California, at the Rocketdyne Division of Rockwell International. This company has been building rocket engines since 1955. Every U.S. manned space launch except one has used Rocketdyne engines.

The spacecraft is largely operated by computers. The engines are controlled with a throttle, and every valve is checked and tested fifty times a second to make sure the rocket runs smoothly.

Five computers control and keep watch on all systems aboard the shuttle. Astronauts can use these computers to send reports. The computers also guide the shuttle during liftoff and reentry.

SIX PARTS TO A MISSION

There are six important phases to each space shuttle mission:

1. LAUNCH—The space shuttle rises from the launch pad powered by more than 7 million pounds (3.15 million kg) of thrust from three main rocket engines and two solid-rocket booster engines.

2. SEPARATION—Two minutes, twelve seconds after launch, the spacecraft reaches a height of 30 miles (48 km) and is traveling at over 2,900 miles (4,640 km) an hour. The solid rockets shut down, separate, and parachute into the ocean. They are picked up by a ship and brought back to Cape Canaveral to be used again. The main shuttle engines continue firing.

3. TANK JETTISON—Eight minutes, fifty-one seconds after launch, the shuttle is 74 miles (118 km) up and moving at nearly 16,700 miles (26,720) an hour. The fuel tank separates, falls, and burns up in the atmosphere. Small engines are fired to get the craft into low orbit.

4. MISSION TASKS—The shuttle can stay in space for up to thirty days. While in orbit, the astronauts conduct experiments, place satellites in orbit, and run tests on the shuttle's equipment.

5. REENTRY—When the mission is finished, the astronauts fire a rocket, and the spacecraft drops toward the earth at 17,000 miles (27,200 km) an hour. Tiles on the hull glow red from the intense heat.

6. LANDING—Coming in like a glider, the orbiter is guided by the pilot to a smooth landing on the runway.

BEHIND THE SCENES

When we think of space travel, we usually think of the astronauts first. But there are thousands of other people who contribute to making missions into space possible. Most of them work behind the scenes. They are the scientists, engineers, and researchers at the leading space laboratories in the United States. These laboratories include:

The Johnson Space Center. This large collection of buildings laid out on Texas ranchland near Galveston

**The launch
of the
*Columbia***

This photograph of the *Columbia*'s second ascent into space was taken by astronaut John Young, a member of the crew on the *Columbia*'s maiden voyage. At the time this picture was snapped, Young was flying in a shuttle training aircraft.

The *Columbia* prepares to land. Note the T-38 "chase plane" nearby, keeping an eye on the progress of the orbiter.

Bay has been the setting for some very important, history-making events. The first flight to the moon was directed from there. Mission Control, the important guiding force for all manned spaceflights, is located in one of the buildings. Scientists and engineers developed the shuttle at this space center. And the growing corps of American astronauts are trained there.

"The people look very ordinary if you watch them come through the gate," said one aerospace employee, "but they are extraordinary in intellectual capacity and drive." Everyone at Johnson seems to work to the limit of their ability. In fact, some people work such long, intense hours that after a while they just "burn out." They end up quitting and going on to some quieter job. According to one official, "burnout" seems to be higher in the space program than in routine jobs "because there is very little about NASA that is routine."

There are shopping centers, hospitals, a graduate university, and many housing projects nearby. Public schools there are said to be among the best in the country. As the space program grew, so did the Johnson Space Center. More than 50,000 people, many working for NASA, have located in that area within the last twenty years.

The Marshall Space Flight Center. Thirty years ago, Huntsville, Alabama, was a small farming community. Today, it is one of the world's most advanced technology centers. And the population has grown from 17,000 in 1950 to more than 200,000 in 1982.

Marshall Space Flight Center focuses on the future. Engineers there are developing the Space Telescope, a space laboratory, and new ways to make metals, crystals, and medicines in orbit. Like the scientists and technicians at Houston, they are very dedicated to their work.

"You come in on a Saturday, and there'll be lots of cars in the parking lot," said one NASA executive. "The lights burn late, too. And it's usually on their own time." Scientists at Marshall are making plans for the utilization of space that could completely change life on earth as we know it.

Above: an aerial view of the Johnson Space Center in Houston, Texas. *Below:* an aerial view of the Marshall Space Flight Center in Huntsville, Alabama.

The Kennedy Space Center. A flat patch of sand on Merritt Island in Cape Canaveral, Florida, is the setting for America's most famous "space port." It is also the home of the shuttle launch pad.

More than 12,000 workers are involved in putting the shuttle together and launching it. "If we start having dozens of shuttle flights a year, as they hope," says Joe Smith of the Chamber of Commerce, "it'll be like an airport."

Kennedy space employees are working toward that goal. They have built a landing strip for the shuttle and put together equipment for moving the orbiter about. And they've been developing a system for reducing launch turnaround time from months to a few weeks.

LIFE ABOARD THE SHUTTLE

From space center to launching pad, launching pad into orbit—what then? Space fans are as interested in the details of everyday life aboard the shuttle as they are in the technology that made it possible. What's it like up there? What do the astronauts eat? What do they do? What do they talk about?

A morning on earth isn't the same as a morning in space. Jack Lousma, flying the third shuttle mission in March 1982, explained it this way, as he talked to controllers in Houston: "It's been an interesting morning to wake up," he said. "It was beautiful and sunny. We pulled up the window shade and looked out. Halfway through the pass, the sun went down, and now it's black as night. I guess we'll go back to bed," he joked. A "pass" is astronaut talk for one complete orbit of the earth, which takes only an hour and a half.

After their morning wake-up call, the crew usually checks their daily schedule on the teleprinter. Breakfast is next. If they're starved, the astronauts may grab a handful of cookies and peanuts. But if they're willing to wait, sometimes an hour or more, they can sit down to a big breakfast of sausage, eggs, diet peaches, granola, orange juice, and a roll. Large meals take longer to fix because the dehydrated food has to be rehydrated first and then warmed. In other words, the food comes dried, and the moisture must be put back in it before heating and eating.

Pad A, Launch Complex 39, at the Kennedy
Space Center in Florida. This pad has been
the site for all space shuttle launchings.

Astronaut Jack Lousma on the third shuttle mission. He is seen here at the commander's station on the flight deck of the *Columbia*.

Astronauts Donald Williams and Rhea Seddon
prepare a meal in the space shuttle 1-G trainer
laboratory at the Johnson Space Center. Both
are rehydrating food packets.

Above: Todd Nelson (center) explaining his "bug-box" experiment to the astronauts who will tend to it in orbit. *Below:* Astronaut Gordon Fullerton checking on the box in space.

Advanced models of the shuttle will take care of this inconvenience, however. Future astronauts will be able to prepare their food in a streamlined kitchen, or galley, like the ones found on airliners.

ALL IN A DAY'S WORK

Some astronauts munch part of their meal while they begin the day's work. This work includes running and keeping a watch on the various scientific experiments aboard. One experiment on the third shuttle mission resulted from the Student Involvement Project.

Eighteen-year-old science student Todd Nelson sent up a collection of flying insects to see how they would survive in microgravity. He called his experiment "Insects in Flight Motions Study."

Commander Jack Lousma and pilot C. Gordon Fullerton showed the experiment on national television. "They sure do make noise," Lousma quipped. "It's hard to sleep at night with them buzzing away. The moths are lively, the bees have gotten stationary, and the flies took to walking. The bees got smart fast," he added. "They decided there wasn't any use flapping their wings and going out of control, so they just float around and wiggle their legs."

HOUSEKEEPING, TOO!

In space, nothing is routine. Something as simple as dumping excess water can be a big deal! On one flight, a toilet needed fixing and a window got fogged up. Hitting a switch by accident is another common problem. In low gravity, a floating body can hit a button or latch unexpectedly. To keep an accident from happening, the important buttons are rimmed with metal or protected with a plastic cover.

A NIGHT IN SPACE

While in flight, the crew follows the same time schedule as Houston. Thus, when night falls in Texas, the astronauts put away their day's work and get ready for seven or eight hours of sleep.

Not all of them can fall asleep right away, however. Some lie awake for a while and sightsee. "Colors are even more colorful from up here," reported Jack Lousma, "because you can see them all together . . . snow-covered mountains and circular-shaped irrigated fields—all different colors, like a patchwork quilt."

[45

4

ASTRONAUT IN TRAINING

Can't you just see it? *Outer Space News, The Daily Space Gazette, Space Times,* or some other newspaper of the future may carry these routine ads—"HELP WANTED: Doctors, lawyers, mechanics, farmers, and hotel managers to work in space. Transportation provided."

It may sound like a fantasy now, but before long it could be real. For many years it was enough for one or two people at a time to go into space and return again. Now the shuttle flights are preparing the way for thousands of people to begin working there.

THE SPACE SHUTTLE CREW Besides the pilot and copilot, who fly the spacecraft, there are two other positions available. Payload specialists are experts in operating the sophisticated equipment that is carried into space in the shuttle's cargo bay. This could be an experiment that is to take place inside the shuttle itself or a satellite to be placed in space.

Payload specialists might make only one trip, depending on the equipment involved. Their training would be brief. They would not be full-time astronauts.

Mission specialists, however, are professional astronauts. They spend most of their work time in space or in preparing to go into space. Some, like Sally Ride and the other women in training, will operate various systems aboard the shuttle.

SPECIAL TRAINING No matter what their job, all shuttle crew members will learn many new skills. Astronauts-in-training are taught how to escape from the spacecraft during an emergency, how to survive on land and water, how to run certain kinds of experiments, and how to operate the shuttle itself.

As part of their two- or three-year training program, the astronaut-trainees attend classes. They study manuals and listen to other astronauts tell about their experiences and problems encountered during practice and real flights.

Before they can actually go into space, the astronauts must learn how to live in a nearly weightless, or low-g, environment. They train in a huge 25-foot-deep (7.5-m) pool called the "water immersion facility." This gives them the chance to experience the feelings of free body movement ("free-fall") that they will have in space. During this part of the training, they practice such things as drinking, eating, and using various kinds of equipment in free-fall.

The new astronauts also learn how to handle the shuttle's many controls and systems. They practice in special cockpits that look exactly like the real thing. These simulators were specially built for use in training.

In the motion base simulator, astronauts feel the motion of the spacecraft as well as hear the sounds of the ship during lift-off and landing. In the shuttle mission simulator, they learn about the rest of the flight.

Outside the windows are pictures of what the earth looks like from space. The astronaut-trainees operate real equipment during simulation exercises—and sometimes make real and costly mistakes!

MAKING THE TEAM When NASA is ready to train a new class of astronauts, they make a public announcement. Thousands of men and women apply for these jobs. NASA then decides how many people they will need from this list. All of those chosen already have college degrees and other specialized training. They must also pass difficult physical tests, including vision and hearing exams.

Young people visiting the Johnson Space Center

Sally Ride, during survival exercises, learned how to eject herself from a disabled shuttle and land safely using a parachute.

Sally Ride preparing to be hoisted into
the air by a parasail. This will simulate
the sensation of a parachute glide.

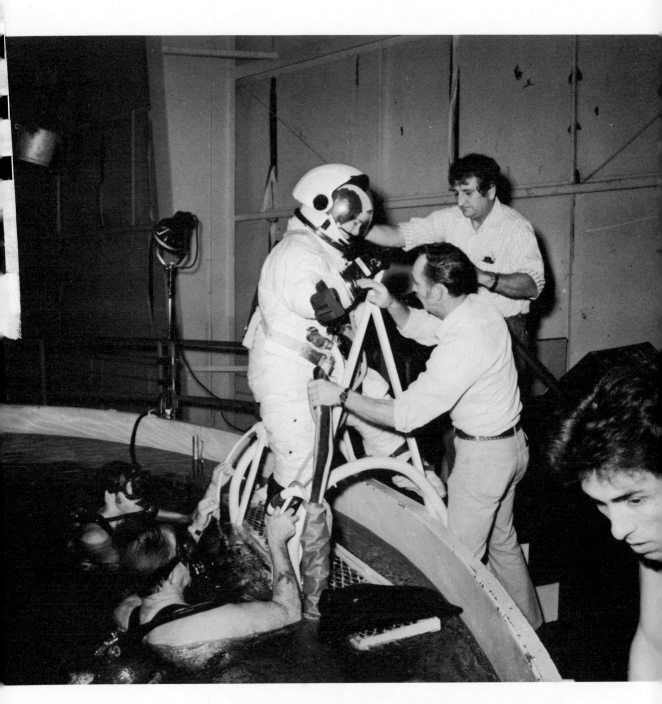

Anna Fisher, wearing a pressurized space suit,
descends into the water immersion facility
at the Johnson Space Center.

often ask, "Can I become an astronaut?" Here are some of the requirements involved:

Age: under 40
Height: 60 to 74 inches (150 to 185 cm)
Eyesight: 20/100 and correctable to 20/20
Education: college degree in science or engineering; some flying experience preferred.

Candidates are also given psychological tests. First, they take a series of written tests. Then two psychiatrists interview them. Anyone with serious mental problems is not allowed to go any further in the program. At a later point, the trainees are again interviewed, but this time by a special group of astronauts, doctors, and people working in flight operations. This board of experts scores each man or woman on his or her education, health, character, performance (how he or she does in front of the group), and interest in the program. The interview lasts about forty-five minutes.

Persistence—hanging in there—is important. More than half of the astronauts selected in 1980 had been turned down in 1978. Anna Fisher's husband, Bill, was one. And Mike Collins, who flew on the historic *Apollo II* moon mission, was rejected twice before he became an astronaut.

Before applying a second time, Bill Fisher went back to school and earned another degree. In addition to his M.D., he got a master's degree in engineering.

WHAT DOES IT TAKE?

Pilots. Those who want to fly the shuttle need a college degree (B.A.) in engineering, biology, physics, or mathematics. An advanced degree (M.A. or Ph.D.) and working experience is also preferred. In addition, pilot candidates must have at least one thousand hours of being in command of a jet aircraft. And those who have experience as a test pilot have an even better chance.

Mission Specialists. People interested in this job need the same college degrees as pilots. In addition, they must have some biological science and at least three years of working experience in their special field of study.

Sally Ride, for example, worked for three years in X-ray astrophysics at Stanford University. Rhea Seddon had four years of training and experience in surgery after she got her degree. And Anna Fisher worked as an emergency-room physician.

As part of their training, Anna and Rhea, both medical doctors, rode in rescue helicopters. They had on board the best emergency equipment available. "In training exercises," said Rhea, "we try to simulate situations that could actually happen. We 'rescue' uniformed dummies, perform emergency procedures on them in shaky, noisy helicopters, and then get them to our back-up trauma centers."

The two young doctors also practiced giving medical care at launchings and landings. If anything goes wrong at either time, they will be ready to put their special training to use.

Payload Specialists. When a satellite is carried into space on the shuttle, specialists from the company that manufactured it may go along. These technical experts will receive most of their training from the company.

They will also receive about one hundred and fifty hours at the Johnson Space Center. This training will include learning about the shuttle and the equipment used to support the payload. It will also include taking part in housekeeping and other duties on board, as well as learning what to do in case of an emergency.

BACK TO SCHOOL Shortly after a new team of astronauts is selected, they head for the classroom. It's back to studying basic science and math, plus courses in meteorology (the study of weather), guidance and navigation, astronomy, physics, and computers.

Special clothing must be worn during the trip into space. In addition, the pressurized space suits may be needed in emergencies and must be used for "space walks." Therefore, the astronauts wear them during many hours of mission training.

Shuttle pilots need to practice landing the spacecraft on a runway, so they will be ready when the real landing takes place. For this, they use simulators and other aircraft during training.

The astronauts have other responsibilities, too. They must keep informed about the spacecraft, payload, and any new developments in the launching equipment or procedure. This requires them to attend many special meetings at the space center.

No one astronaut can know everything there is to know. So each is given a different area to learn about. From time to time, individual astronauts give reports to the whole group so that everyone can be kept up-to-date on what is happening.

SHAPING UP FOR SPACE

Before their final selection, the astronaut-trainees are put through some pretty tough physical-fitness tests. "We literally ran until we couldn't run anymore," said Mary Cleave. They are also hooked up to special machines to measure their breathing and heart rates under stress. "They tested our strength," said Mary, "and generally made sure we were healthy. Then, once we were selected, it was up to us to stay at that level of fitness."

There is no regular daily exercise routine for the astronauts. "We just work it into our schedules," said Mary. But each of them knows the importance of being in good condition. From time to time they are given a physical exam to make sure they have remained fit.

How do some of the female astronauts stay in shape? Many work out at the gym that is available at the space center. Others run, jog, or play a sport.

Sally Ride, for example, has always been athletic. "I run a couple of miles or play tennis every day," she told one reporter. Judith Resnick, Rhea Seddon, and Anna Fisher also jog. Kathryn Sullivan runs and plays racquetball. And when she has time, she goes sailing and even enters sailing races.

Keeping fit while in space is also important, say NASA medical experts. Because of the low gravity, the heart doesn't have to pump as hard in space, so it can get out of shape easily. To stay fit while aboard the shuttle,

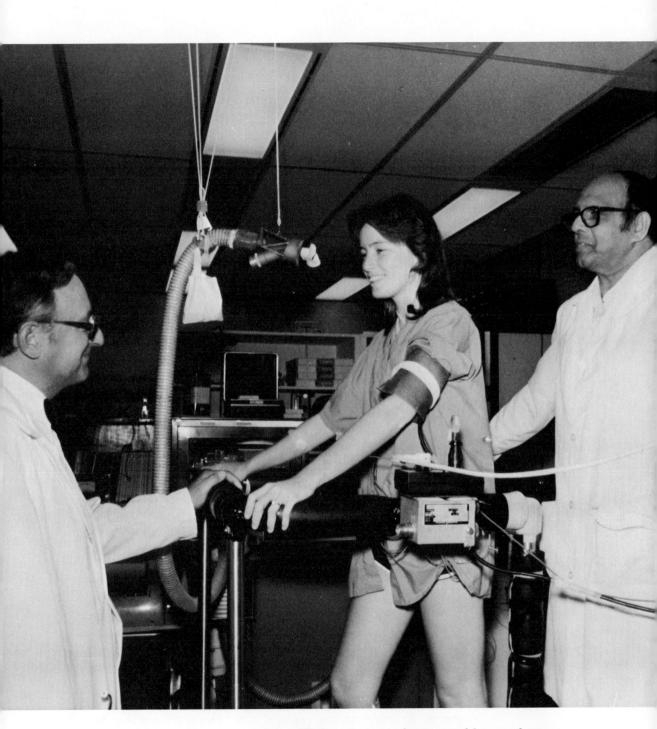

Anna Fisher is seen here working out on a
treadmill device at the Johnson Space Center.

astronauts use a new treadmill, built specially for low-g use.

FLIGHT ASSIGNMENTS When an astronaut is assigned to a particular flight, his or her schedule gets very crowded. Sally Ride now knows just how crowded. To get ready for her first flight, she took part in what is called "mission specific training."

"We'll be trying to assimilate the entire flight in advance by computer," Sally told a reporter for the *Saturday Evening Post.* "This is intense training. We'll aim to be prepared for anything that might come up."

In the space shuttle program, flights will be frequent, and crews will be named well ahead of the launch date. As a result, several crews will be in training at the same time.

Each crew will receive "cross-training" so that at least one person can handle the duties of all the others. Some flights will also have a backup crew. These men and women will go through the same training as the original crew. In case of accident or illness, any crew member can then easily be replaced without having to cancel the mission. Each crew also takes part in spacecraft reviews and test programs so they can stay familiar with the shuttle and its systems.

Things move even more quickly when the astronauts begin working with the simulators. First they must learn the individual tasks for their particular mission and how to fly the spacecraft. Then they practice putting all the various activities together in the order they will be carried out during the real flight.

Simulators provide the astronauts with very realistic settings for their work. Views of the earth, stars, payloads, and landing runway are projected onto screens where the windows would be. This gives the crew a good idea of what to expect. In fact, some of them come back from their mission feeling like they had made the same flight many times before.

Several weeks before lift-off, the training reaches a peak. At this time the mission simulator is linked with Mission Control and the simulated tracking stations. Crews and flight controllers practice the whole mission from start to finish to make sure everything is ready for the real flight.

Between training sessions, crew members continue learning about the spacecraft and the payloads for their mission. They also practice conducting experiments and deploying or recovering satellites or other payloads in space. They handle and operate various pieces of equipment. While all this is going on, the astronauts must also keep themselves physically and mentally fit for their mission.

When the flight is finished, their job is still not over. Crew members spend several hours or days debriefing—reporting their experiences so that future crews will know what worked and what didn't work. These sessions help NASA planners determine whether spacecraft systems, payload handling, or even training procedures need to be improved. News reporters are also anxious to talk to the astronauts after they have completed a flight, so they can report the events to their viewers and readers. Then, after a short vacation, astronauts return to their jobs, where studies and training begin again for the next lift-off into the heavens.

5

TRAVEL GEAR FOR OUTER SPACE

Mattresses and pillows are out. Liquid salt and pepper are in. Chili is off the list of favorite foods. Meat with gravy is on.

These are just a few of the things shuttle astronauts must adjust to as they journey from earth to the region we call space.

WORK OR PLAY Space is a region where the temperatures of objects routinely move from −250° Fahrenheit (−157°C) to 250°F (121°C), where gravity barely exists, and where the atmosphere is almost a total vacuum. Why would anyone want to go to such a place?

To men and women with the spirit and courage of a Christopher Columbus or a Marco Polo, it's an exciting adventure. If earthbound explorers thought they had problems with food, clothing, and equipment, however, space pioneers have them beat.

Living in space is no small feat. In fact, modern-day scientists and engineers work long hours to provide the astronauts with all the comforts of home—well, almost all of them. Surviving in a world of near-zero gravity does have its challenges . . .

SEASON TO TASTE When an astronaut says, "Please pass the salt," he or she won't receive the usual glass shaker. Ordinary crystal grains of salt are almost impossible to use in space. They won't shake out. And if a few particles do escape, they tend to drift off in space. Instead, salt, pepper, and other spices come in liquid form.

Foods taste different in space, too. Crews noticed that most of their meals lacked flavor. The reason for this may be that in low-g, body fluids tend to move toward the upper half of the body. This results in a feeling of a stuffed-up nose and blocked sinuses, which may cause a numbing of the senses of taste and smell.

"It feels pretty much like you have a cold all the time," reported astronaut Gerald Carr, commander of the third *Skylab* mission. *Skylab* was a U.S. space station that was launched into orbit in 1973 and was visited by three teams of astronauts before it fell to earth in 1979.

To spice things up a bit, space shuttle food cabinets will now be stocked with liquid and dehydrated garlic and hot sauce.

HOLD THE CHILI! During the *Skylab* missions, astronauts crossed chili off their list in a hurry. Every time they opened a container of this spicy dish, the food exploded. "Great goblets of chili go flying all over; it's bad news," reported the crew.

Meals with sauces or gravies, however, tend to stick to the plate instead of floating away. Even in low gravity these foods can be eaten on an open plate with a fork or spoon.

Meals are put together carefully—piece by piece. Before all flights, the food is precooked and then canned, dehydrated (moisture removed), or packed in aluminum-lined plastic envelopes called flex pouches.

To return the moisture to the dehydrated food, the crew uses a needle to squirt water into the sealed pouches. Each pouch has a flexible plastic top so that the "chef" can knead or work the water into the food with his or her hands.

Why do it this way? Because in low-g you can't simply pour water from a pitcher or glass. It will break up into silvery little balls and drift around the spacecraft. So when the astronauts want some water, coffee, or juice, they must drink it in a pouch through a straw with a clamp attached to it. The clamp keeps the straw pinched shut when the astronaut is not drinking.

Space meals are carefully planned and carefully put together. Here, Rhea Seddon, in the Johnson 1-G trainer laboratory, arranges food items in a portable food warmer.

Seddon now arranges the dinner items on a food tray attached to a locker door. The items are held in place by springs and Velcro tape.

All foods and liquids come in containers shaped to fit slots on a specially built, magnetized food tray. The containers are held in place by Velcro tape.

KEEPING CLEAN

Since water is hard to hold onto in space, keeping clean can pose a bit of a problem. Fans are used in water drains when astronauts wash so the water can't escape.

Using the toilet is a new adventure, too. The space shuttle's toilet has a footrest, a handhold, and a seat belt to hold the crew member in place. Suction pumps take the place of flushing.

Showering in previous missions used to take a lot of time. To clean up, bathers had to squirt their bodies with a water gun. Meanwhile, a partner stood nearby with a small vacuum cleaner ready to suck in the escaping droplets of water.

A better method is now being developed. One planner has suggested a kind of "human car wash." Space bathers would step into a sealed box, be sprayed with water, then be completely air-dried.

SLUMBER PARTY IN SPACE

In space, where almost nothing is routine, bedtime seems to be a fairly simple matter. Each astronaut steps into a sleeping bag that is held fast to a firm surface, zips the bag from toe to chest, connects a waist strap, and tucks both arms under the strap to keep them from floating upward during sleep.

The shuttle's sleeping area looks like a two-level bunk bed. One astronaut sleeps on the top, a second on the bottom, and a third one underneath the bottom bunk, facing the floor.

Without gravity, sleepers could actually be comfortable in any position—standing up or lying down. Pillows and mattresses aren't necessary, either. A padded board works just fine.

ON THE MOVE

Skylab astronauts kept in shape by riding a stationary bicycle and walking on a specially built treadmill. There is no room for the bicycle aboard the shuttle, but the crew can tone up on the treadmill.

One problem space athletes face is perspiration. It

Astronaut Henry Hartsfield, Jr., demonstrates the sleeping accommodations aboard the *Columbia*.

Astronaut Joe Engle works out on the new treadmill aboard the *Columbia*.

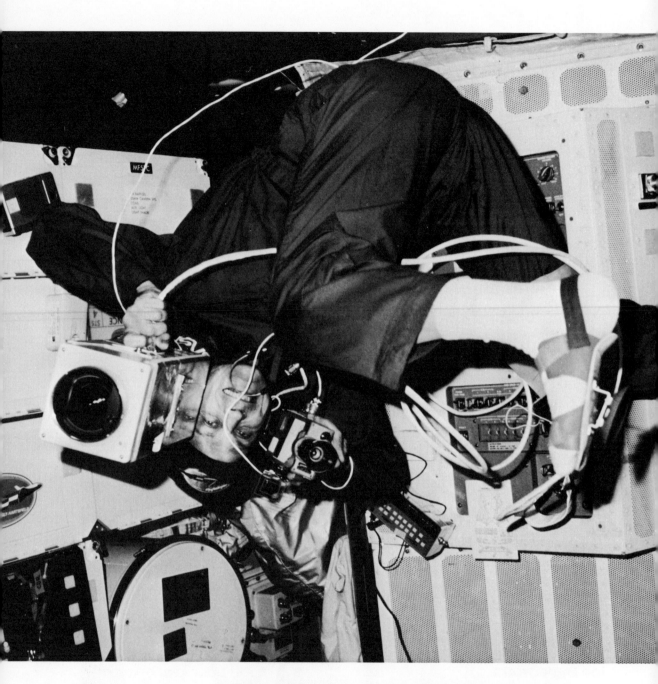

Because of the low gravity, standing still in space is very hard to do. Astronaut Thomas Mattingly II, during the fourth flight of the *Columbia*, shows off the latest in space fashion—suction-cup footwear.

doesn't simply dry and disappear. It hangs around and sticks to the skin, layer upon layer. A small fan helped the *Skylab* crew blow it off their bodies. Then the unwanted sheets of perspiration had to be vacuumed out of the air.

Because of the low gravity, standing still is as impossible in space as flying is on the ground. Astronauts in the shuttle attach suction-cup soles to their shoes when they want to stay in one spot. Without something to hold them in place, the crew wouldn't get much done.

One time, astronaut William Pogue in *Skylab* forgot to anchor himself as he tried to unscrew a bolt. When he turned the screwdriver, he suddenly corkscrewed through the air with it.

Without even trying, an astronaut can look just like a gymnast. Unless there is something to brace oneself against, even a simple motion like bending over can turn into a somersault. To eliminate these problems, the astronauts have portable handholds with suction cups that can be used almost anywhere on the shuttle.

SPACE FURNITURE

Without gravity, humans cannot really sit down. So furniture has to be designed to fit the stoop, or slouch, that seems natural for a body in space.

In order to stay seated at a table the way earthlings do, the nearly weightless crew would have to keep their stomach muscles tensed. Tables and control panels in former flights were too low for the upward-drifting astronauts.

Shuttle furniture will solve that problem. Tables for working and eating are about a foot (.3 m) higher than those used on earth. And their metal surfaces are just right for holding magnetic paperweights and food trays.

THE WELL-DRESSED ASTRONAUT

For 115-pound (51.75-kg) Sally Ride or Mary Cleave, who weighs less than 100 pounds (45 kg), suiting up for space could be quite a chore. The basic outfit weighs more than most of its wearers!

The new computerized space suits—Extravehicular Mobility Units (EMUs), as they're officially called—were designed to wear outside the spacecraft. These amaz-

Astronaut Bruce McCandless II demonstrates the newest manned maneuvering unit (MMU) and space suit to be used for all future extravehicular activities (EVA) in space.

ing outfits will keep the astronauts alive and protected as they repair and deploy satellites, do experiments in space, and take care of housekeeping tasks.

With the necessary backpack, which holds a portable life-support system (PLSS), the suit weighs 234 pounds (105.3 kg). Attach the manned maneuvering unit (MMU) to the backpack so that the astronauts can power themselves around in space, and the suit weighs 250 pounds (112.5) more. But, of course, none of this means anything in the near weightlessness of space!

ONE FOR ALL The *Apollo* astronauts wore custom-built space suits. But the new model is designed for everyone. By combining different parts—arms, upper-body section, pants, gloves, and boots—many variations are possible.

The old suits took more than an hour to put on. And the astronauts had to help each other get in and out of them. With the new version, the shuttle crew can dress and undress themselves in a matter of minutes.

After the suit is in place, the cooling system is turned on, sending chilled water through tiny tubes in the special full-length underwear. This system protects the astronaut from the sun's heat. Next comes the air. It flows in over the head and down into the suit, then back up and out. In space, pure oxygen is used. Within five minutes the entire suit is pressurized. A special rack supports the weight of the backpack and the space suit itself.

The portable life-support system, in the backpack, supplies seven hours of oxygen—for breathing, pressurizing the suit, and cooling. For added protection, there's a second pack that can supply another half-hour of emergency oxygen.

The backpack also carries a two-way radio. Inside the plastic bubble helmet there are two microphones and a set of earphones. The helmet also has a gold-plated visor to protect the eyes.

A small display and control module (DCM) sits on the upper chest portion of the suit. With just a push of a button, the astronauts can control water flow, fan, radio, or any other items they need.

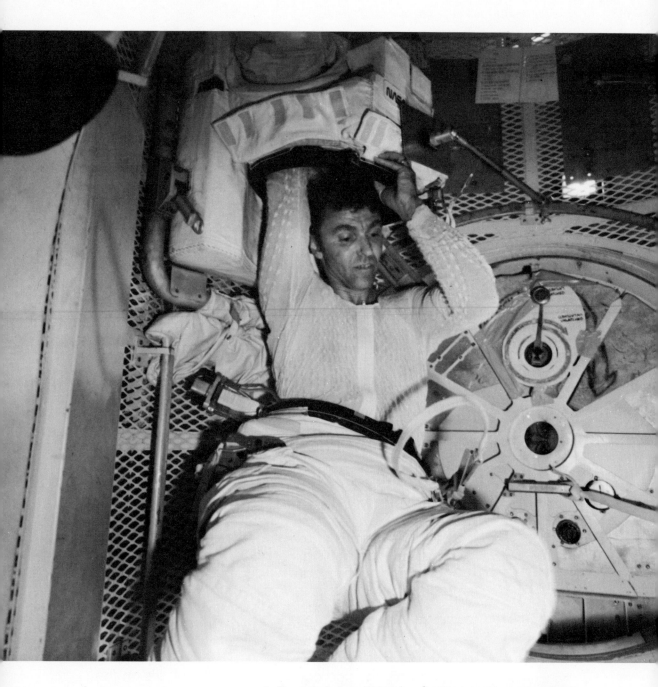

Astronaut Joe Engle practices donning and doffing his extravehicular mobility unit (EMU) aboard a KC-135 "zero-gravity" aircraft.

Astronauts can also receive messages on a special display unit that is hooked up to a thumb-size microprocessor in the backpack. This display can alert them to a problem with the suit and give immediate instructions on how to correct the problem.

Electric power for the suits comes mainly from the shuttle's airlock compartment. In addition, a 9.8-pound (4.41-kg) silver-zinc battery can be used for power outside the shuttle.

STRANGE EFFECTS During the *Skylab* mission, when space crews lived in low-g for one to three months, a curious discovery was made. The astronauts had trouble getting into their space suits. They claimed the suits were too tight. NASA didn't understand the complaint. The suits had been custom-made for each man and carefully checked before lift-off.

When the astronauts returned to earth, the mystery cleared up. The men had "grown" while in space—some as much as two inches. NASA calls this "in-flight growth." In a nearly weightless atmosphere, the spinal column becomes relaxed and stretches. There is no gravity to compress the soft disks between the spinal bones, so bodies expand and grow—at least temporarily.

To solve this problem, suits for the space shuttle astronauts were designed to "grow" with their wearers. The new suits now have laced-in sections in the legs and sleeves. As the astronaut grows, he or she can let out the suit a little at a time, as needed.

Not only do low-g bodies grow, they change shape as well. Because body fluids move upwards in space, astronauts notice that their chests and shoulders become slightly larger. And since there is less fluid below, waists appear narrower and feet thinner. To take care of this, space suits now have a jacket with built-in elasticized pleats that expand with the body.

When the astronauts return to earth, the fluids flow back down in a hurry. The drop can be so sudden that it can cause the person to black out. To avoid this, astronauts now wear special leggings, or antigravity pants, for reentry. The pants can be inflated to put pressure on the lower body and thus slow down the flow of fluids.

Space suits are expensive. So far NASA has spent several million dollars on the development of the latest suits alone. But without proper gear, venturing out into space would be impossible. As important as the shuttle is, the space program could not go very far without these amazing outfits.

THE SKY'S THE LIMIT–
A GLIMPSE INTO THE FUTURE

How would you like to go to school or work fewer hours each week? Have more time for hobbies and fun? Travel across the United States in half the time it now takes? Ride in an underground pipeline?

During the next hundred years, people may be living much like that. The discoveries we make through our nation's space program will affect every area of our lives. Men and women will work eighteen hours a week instead of forty. They'll have more leisure time for outside interests. Travel will be faster. And energy will be cheap and plentiful.

These are just some of the things being planned for citizens of the twenty-first century, says Gerard K. O'Neill, a physics professor at Princeton University. Dr. O'Neill is president of the Space Studies Institute. He also writes articles and books about the future.

ROUTINE TRIPS INTO SPACE In an interview published in *U.S. News & World Report* in 1981, O'Neill talked about how he expects the space program to change our lives. Space colonies will exist in the foreseeable future, he feels. "By 2081, 200 million people will be making routine trips into space and back every year," he said. Others will actually live there, returning to earth for an occasional visit.

Spaceships in the future will fly about 300 miles (480 km) per second. This is a big improvement over past flights. Just thirteen years ago, *Apollo* astronauts

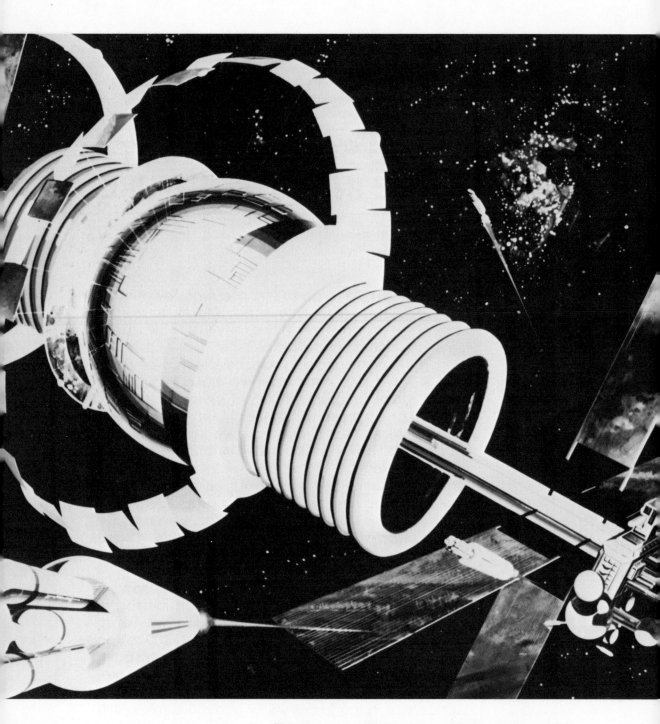

This is one artist's view of the exterior of a possible space habitat for 10,000 people.

returned from the moon at only 6 miles (9.6 km) per second.

Space colonies will be built close together, for easier telephone communications. The energy they need will come directly from the sun shining on very thin mirrors made of aluminum. By rotating the colonies, they could have artificial gravity similar to gravity on earth. This would enable them to hold onto an atmosphere. Space citizens could then grow the same grass, trees, flowers, and crops that we have on earth.

SMALL TOWNS —IN SPACE AND ON EARTH

It will be easier and cheaper to build several small space colonies rather than one large one. This is something people on earth will probably want to imitate within the next century, says O'Neill.

O'Neill feels that people get along best when they live and work in small groups of ten thousand or so. Crime and warfare seem to come about when cities reach a million or more.

Earth communities of the future will provide comfortable living year-round. Each one will have its own retractable roof that will be opened or closed, depending on the weather outside. This will give people the freedom to jog, bicycle, or play ball whenever they want to.

More people will work at home during the next century. They can stay in touch with their offices by computer. This will make taking care of young children easier. And computers will also make it easier to do one's job. Extensive paper filing can be eliminated, and workers can send information electronically instead of using the mail or a messenger service.

People will also work fewer hours each week. Citizens of the future will probably put as much time into their hobbies as they put into their jobs—maybe even more.

FLOATING INSTEAD OF DRIVING

Long-distance travel will also be more common in the future. Families will be able to visit relatives and friends in other parts of the country more cheaply and use less travel time. For example, kids living in Chicago could make a trip to New York in half an hour, have dinner with their grandparents, go to a movie or concert, and return home the same evening. But how?

A new form of transportation may turn long-distance trips into short hops. The "floater" system will carry people in vehicles that move in a vacuum tube underground. Such systems could be built without interfering with the land now used for highways. Travel will be faster than the speed of sound. People will be able to go from New York to Washington, D.C., in just fourteen minutes.

One hundred years from now, people will have cars and aircraft, as we do now. But drivers will no longer have to sit stuck in traffic jams for hours. Twenty-first-century vehicles will be guided by computers that obey voice commands.

THE AMAZING SPACE VAN

Space vehicles will also continue to improve. One that is planned for the near future is called the "space van." This small orbiter will be owned and operated by a private company and used to haul cargo to and from space. It will look very much like a mini-version of NASA's space shuttle.

The space van would ride atop a 747 for takeoff from a large airfield. When the 747 reached an altitude of 40,000 feet (12,000 m), the smaller aircraft would separate from it. The space van pilot would then fire the orbiter's six rockets, and the craft would blast into space. Within minutes this small shuttle would be in orbit 280 miles (448 km) above the earth.

The idea for the space van was developed by an aerospace engineer named Len Cormier. He and others believe that space transportation will soon become big business. Cormier feels that in order to be successful, his space van must provide customers with a less expensive ride than the shuttle. So he is doing all he can to keep the costs as low as possible. The space van, for example, will not have all the comforts of the shuttle because its main purpose will be to carry cargo. To some it will be a kind of U-Haul for the space age.

The mini-orbiter is about ready to go into production. But it takes money to manufacture it—lots of money.

Cormier says he needs $500 million to produce the first three. Eventually, he'd like to have a fleet of thirty or more.

SERVICE STATION IN THE SKY

NASA continues to plan for the future, too. Right now, engineers, scientists, and designers are studying the possible development of a permanent "service station" in space. According to a report put out by the Johnson Space Center, the SOC (Space Operations Center) would operate continuously. Parts for the center would be delivered and put together by the shuttle orbiter, which would carry into orbit huge cylinders and some service units. They would be lifted from the shuttle's cargo bay and connected in space.

The cylinders would serve as the command control center, the housekeeping quarters, and the laboratory. Passageways would connect these areas. The service module, containing the life-support systems, power unit, communications equipment, an airlock, and a docking berth or landing place for the shuttle, would be set below the cylinders.

SOC would have a crew of two or three persons at first, then four to six. Eventually, it would hold eight to twelve people. Crews would take turns. No one member would stay on the station for more than ninety days.

Cozy Quarters. The living quarters, or habitation modules, could provide the crew with a cozy home away from home. Each one would include sleeping areas, equipment for fixing meals, dining tables, lighting, exercise equipment, and storage areas. SOC will also have bathroom facilities and a kitchen for preparing frozen foods, a folding desk, and an area for recreation.

Health care is also included in the plans for SOC. Habitation module 1 will have equipment similar to a doctor's office. Habitation module 2 will be something like a hospital emergency room. And all the modules will have medical kits for emergencies.

Astronauts would fly to SOC in the space shuttle, carrying their tools and "hard hats" with them. Nearly 300

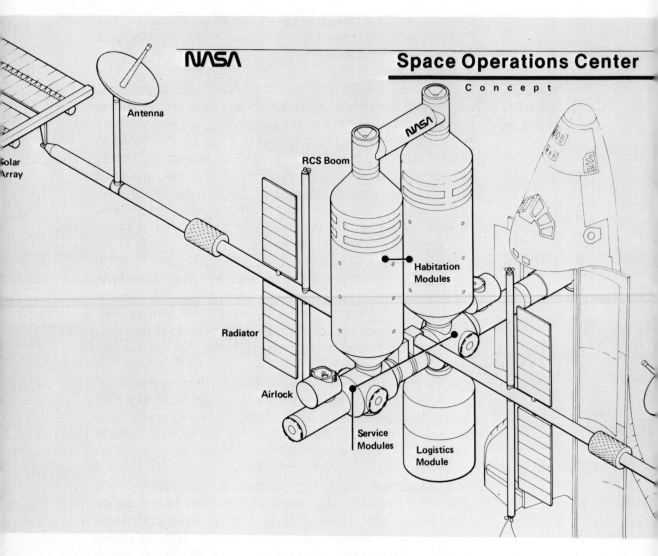

Antenna

Solar Array

RCS Boom

Habitation Modules

Radiator

Airlock

Service Modules

Logistics Module

The Space Operations Center (SOC) concept. *Opposite:* an artist's depiction of SOC as it might look when partially completed. The enclosed space hangar (lower right), docked to a command module, would protect space vehicles from collisions with meteoroids or floating debris while the vehicles were being serviced.

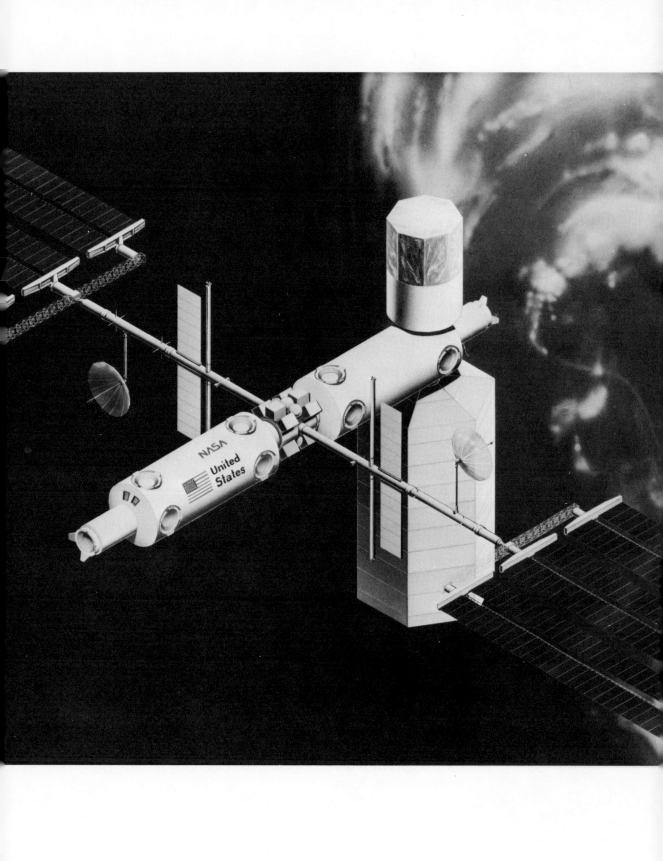

miles (480 km) above the earth, they would begin building huge structures out of thin metal beams. Some workers would zip around with rockets on their backs. Others would pilot small vehicles that look like cars with mechanical arms. At the end of the day's work, they would exercise, relax, clean up, eat, and go to sleep in a habitation module. Their routine would be similar to that of any working person's on earth.

SUPER-ASTRONAUTS AT WORK

In space, workers may look like Supermen or Bionic Women as they move structures and equipment around with one hand. On the ground, the same work would take a crane.

However, since structures in orbit don't have to support any weight, they can be as delicate and light as a butterfly's wings. They can also grow to fantastic size— bigger than anything we know on earth. Workers can add new sections or modules in any direction, as they are needed.

Astronauts working in space would receive instructions and messages from SOC through voice intercom, closed-circuit TV, and caution and warning signals. No worker would ever be out of touch with the command module while doing his or her job in space.

SOME NEW CHALLENGES

In space there is no wind or rain to slow down construction, as there is on earth. On the other hand, working in space will offer challenges earthlings never have to face. For example, workers need to be tied down even when doing such a routine task as turning a screw. If the worker isn't anchored in place, the screw will turn his or her body right along with it.

Of course, construction workers on earth can't push heavy materials around with bare hands, like their co-workers in the sky can. But in hot weather, they can work bare-chested or in T-shirts as they hammer on a roof or nail large wood planks together. Many even get a head start on their summer tan as they work outdoors.

Space is no place for bare chests and shirt-sleeves. The floating workers of the future must wear heavy space suits that will probably get in the way as they perform delicate tasks.

"If you had five or six pairs of gloves and five or six overcoats on all at once, that's what it feels like with a space suit on," said Alan Bean of NASA, who spent fifty-nine days inside *Skylab*. "Your fingers and arms get tired, so you have to minimize motion. You have to get your body in a position where you can move your hands with the least effort," he added.

The gloves alone are so thick and stiff that the astronauts cannot do any delicate work with their hands. It would probably be something like trying to type while wearing ski gloves!

SUN STORM Most people have been caught in the rain or in a snowstorm. But can you imagine being caught in a sun storm? Some future space workers may have this experience at some point. When working in geosynchronous orbit (22,300 miles, or 35,680 km, high and in a seemingly fixed position above the equator), astronauts will need extra protection from the sun, especially during solar flares. These powerful sun storms can cause radiation sickness after only a few hours of exposure.

To avoid this, astronauts will do some of their work in heavily shielded cars. When a solar flare sends a flash of radiation their way, they will be able to make a quick getaway to a lower orbit.

FAR-OUT PROJECTS Once SOC is operating, NASA could have plenty of new projects to keep the astronauts busy. One might involve placing huge antennas in space. Another might be working with Lunetta, a giant mirror that can collect and reflect sunlight to earth. Lunetta could light hundreds of city streets at night. Its light would also make it possible for rescue teams to work at night in disaster areas.

Another project might be the construction of a group of large solar-power satellites. But it would take six hundred workers to build just one of these and fifty thousand tons of material.

Large communications platforms are also being planned for the near future. In fact, engineers at the Marshall Space Flight Center have been working on this for some time. If placed hundreds of miles above the earth, these platforms could provide better space com-

**An artist's conception of a
giant solar-power satellite**

munication services than have ever been possible before.

Building these platforms would also give more people the chance to work in space. The shuttle would fly all the needed parts to a particular site in orbit. Then the space workers would bolt them together.

For larger structures, one company has developed a machine that can manufacture metal beams in space. The "beam builder" will take in rolls of sheet metal at one end and send out finished beams from the other.

A TOUCH OF SCIENCE FICTION

It's exciting to dream about these towering structures in space and about astronauts zipping around the sky and sleek spacecraft flying through the universe. Many of these future projects are more than a dream, however. Some are just about ready to move off the drawing board into space.

Most of the things mentioned in this chapter are possible. Thanks to Sally Ride and all the adventurous men and women in the space program, we are truly beginning to see that the sky's the limit. We *can* make our dreams come true.

Exploring the universe is no longer something we see only in a science fiction movie or read about in a novel. Our future in space is real. LIke the automobile, the airplane, and the telephone, space technology will change our lives. How we deal with those changes is up to us.

ONE WORLD

As exciting as the space program is, most of us know that our responsibilities as residents of this planet involve more than just participation in that one effort. Millions of people all over the earth believe that our world can someday be one world—and that the gifts of the universe belong to all living creatures. Until we solve our problems on earth and begin to work together for the benefit of all, we cannot truly make space the limitless resource it is.

INDEX

[85